Jacki Cartlidge is a retired academic; her professional interests include: literature, education and psychology, life writing, with a particular focus on childhood relationships, socialisation and development. She has taught at all levels up to post graduate supervision. She has written occasional children's stories for BBC Radio since her early twenties, but this is her first collaboration with the illustrator Karen See.

The Tale of
Nana Noo's
Coat

Illustrated By: Karen See

Jacki Cartlidge

AUSTIN MACAULEY PUBLISHERS™
LONDON • CAMBRIDGE • NEW YORK • SHARJAH

A CIP catalogue record for this title is available from the British Library.

ISBN 9781398405745 (Paperback)
ISBN 9781398418875 (ePub e-book)

www.austinmacauley.com

First Published (2021)
Austin Macauley Publishers Ltd
25 Canada Square
Canary Wharf
London
E14 5LQ

For Amelia, Daniel, Darcy, Harry and Chloe

Thanks to my family members, who are so important in my life, and friends, particularly Wilma Fraser and Lynn Barr, for their support and encouragement at important moments. Finally, thanks to Austin Macauley Publishers for their help and enthusiasm.

Sophie watched Mummy reaching into the back of her wardrobe. They were spending the morning talking about Nana Noo and the ways they could do something special to celebrate her long life. They were both sad that Nana Noo had recently passed but Sophie could not even count up all the years Nana Noo had lived. Mummy pulled out a soft, reddish-brown fur coat. Sophie recognised it as the one she'd seen Nana Noo wear last Christmas. It had been very cold and snow was on the ground when Nana Noo arrived to spend Christmas with them. Sophie could only remember seeing Nana Noo wear it once.

Mummy shook it gently and then removed two shiny wooden balls that were suspended from a ribbon around the neck of the coat hanger.

"What are the wooden balls for, Mummy?" asked Sophie.

"They help protect the coat from moths," Mummy replied.

"Why does it need protecting?" Sophie persisted. Mummy gave a deep sigh and brought the coat over to where Sophie had settled herself on the bed.

"The coat is made from the fur of musquash, and the moths might make holes," explained Mummy.

"Musquash are furry creatures."

Sophie saw Mummy give a gentle shudder and Sophie stretched out her hand to stroke the coat. How soft it was.

"Don't you like it?" asked Sophie.

"I don't like the fact that so many creatures were used to make the coat." Mummy parted the soft fur to show Sophie how the skins had been sewn together.

"Were the animals old?" asked Sophie.

"I don't know," said Mummy. "Maybe, but sometimes, animals were kept and bred to make fur coats. Older animals would not be suitable. Many years ago, people thought it was a great luxury to have a fur coat, they were expensive and some people thought it made them special. This coat is very old, Sophie. Nana Noo did not have it from when it was new, it was given to her by her great-aunt. I expect it could even be 100 years old."

"That's very, very old," said Sophie thoughtfully. "What are you going to do with it?" she asked as Mummy reached for her phone.

Mummy hung the coat on the door and took a picture of it. "I think I'll try to sell it on eBay. I wish I could give it away, but no one wants to wear real fur these days. I couldn't wear it," sighed Mummy, mostly to herself.

"Much as Nana Noo loved it, I feel very sad because we don't have much to remind us of Nana Noo. But I need to get rid of this coat. If we could sell it, we could use the money to do something special to remember Nana Noo."

Sophie thought about Nana Noo. She could not imagine her wanting to wear a coat if animals had been killed to make it. Nana Noo loved animals, she had a cat and a dog, and until Sophie was four, three years ago, Nana Noo had kept hens and, sometimes, fluffy, yellow, tiny chickens.

Sophie remembered she refused to eat any eggs unless she could see the hens running about; Mummy had to drive miles sometimes when Nana Noo stayed so that they could see the hens and collect what she called "really free-range eggs". But as she got older, she could not manage her own hens, and they went to a farm near to Nana Noo's; she had told Sophie that she had been to visit the farm before she would let her hens go.

Now, here was a coat made from dead animals, it didn't sound like Nana Noo at all. It was all very confusing.

"What does a musquash look like, Mummy?"
Mummy took Sophie's hand and they left the bedroom and went to find Mummy's laptop.
"I'm not exactly sure," exclaimed Mummy as she turned the laptop on. Soon, photos of the little furry creatures were on the screen.
They don't look very big, thought Sophie. It must take lots of them to make a coat. She was going to ask Mummy, but as Sophie glanced at her, Mummy looked sadder than ever.
"What else have we got of Nana Noo's?" asked Sophie. Maybe this would cheer Mummy up.

"Well, we haven't got much. There's the bracelet she left for you when you are older. I have a set of earrings, but that's about it. Nana Noo tended to give away or perhaps sell things she wasn't using. She said she didn't like possessing lots of "things". There were some clothes that I've already sent to the charity shop, but they wouldn't take the coat."

Mummy paused and then took a deep breath.

"That's it, eBay it is!" she exclaimed.

She felt a little out of her depth, she hadn't used eBay to sell things before, but she had sent off for items occasionally. She knew Sophie's Uncle Bill spent lots of time buying and selling on eBay.

Oh, why hadn't Nana Noo sold the coat when she could have made some money while it was still acceptable to wear fur? Heaven knows Nana Noo had needed the money. Maybe the coat was very special to Nana Noo. But now, perhaps, it could help them provide some money for a celebration, eBay was the answer.

Together, Mummy and Sophie filled in the online forms for eBay. Mummy read some of the phrases out to Sophie that were suggestions for describing the 'item for sale'. They giggled, none of them seemed to describe Nana Noo's coat and what they knew of its history. Soon, the task was completed, Mummy looked faintly relieved and Sophie wanted to know when they would get a reply.

Sophie did not have to wait long. Two days later, Mummy turned on her laptop to find information from eBay that she had a buyer. Once again, the coat was retrieved from the wardrobe. Mummy said they needed to pack the coat up, but Sophie said, "We don't know where it is going." This was true. Nevertheless, relieved to be despatching the coat to a new home, Mummy made plans to wrap the coat and send it. Mummy bought strong brown paper and tape. She carefully folded the coat, but as she did, one or two of the places where the musquash skins were attached started to come apart.

"Oh, dear!" shouted Mummy. "We can't sell it like this, it doesn't look like the photo or the description." After a few moments' thought, Mummy said, "I'd better inform the buyer that I can't send it."

"What will you say?" asked Sophie.

"Well, I will say exactly what happened," said Mummy.

Two days later, a reply came, telling Mummy to send the coat anyway, it would be mended when it arrived. This reply also had an address and a name. So, Mummy slipped a card in with the coat saying they hoped the new owner would love the coat as much as the last owner had. Mummy and Sophie took the parcel to the post office and they were given a receipt. The coat was going to South Africa. Another two days passed, and when Mummy opened up the laptop, there was a message saying the coat had arrived in South Africa but import duty needed paying. Mummy transferred some money and waited.

Two days later, Mummy received another request for more money. This was unexpected, and as she thought about it, Mummy realised the coat had been sent, and maybe the buyer was not genuine. What was she going to say to Sophie? Nana Noo's coat was gone they had lost the postage, the money from the transfer and the sale of the coat. But worst of all, she had sent Nana Noo's coat into the unknown and now they would not have the money to do the 'special something ' to remember Nana Noo.

Mummy spent several days wondering what to say to Sophie. She contacted the payment authority who confirmed that no money had been received. Mummy also spoke to Uncle Bill, who bought and sold quite frequently on eBay, and when he looked at the emails, he confirmed her worst fears. Apart from the fact that she felt silly, Mummy knew Sophie would be upset, and she could hear Nana Noo's voice in her ear, saying, "You always trust and think the best of people."

Mummy shed a few tears, but then her mother's voice said, "But I always loved that about you."

Mummy spent a few more days wondering what to say to her daughter.

Then, one night, in the early hours, Sophie awoke – very excited and shouting,

"Mummy. Mummy, Nana Noo's coat did not go to the buyer. It's safe! Nobody is wearing it." Sophie had had a dream. Mummy was astonished, she had not yet told Sophie about the internet scam.

"Mummy, I saw lots and lots of musquash, they were running along a riverbank. There was lots of grass and things they liked to eat."

Sophie gasped to take a breath.

"They were squeaking and jumping with joy. Then, they ran into holes in the riverbank.